Unicorn Magic

Dreamspell's
Special Wish

Daisy Meadows

For Beatrice

Special thanks to Adrian Bott

ORCHARD BOOKS

First published in Great Britain in 2020 by The Watts Publishing Group

1 3 5 7 9 10 8 6 4 2

Text copyright © 2020 Working Partners Limited
Illustrations © Orchard Books 2020
Series created by Working Partners Limited

A CIP catalogue record for this book is available from the British Library.

ISBN 978 1 40835 702 6

Printed and bound in Great Britain by Clays Ltd, Elcograf S.p.A.

The paper and board used in this book are made from wood from responsible sources.

Orchard Books
An imprint of Hachette Children's Group
Part of The Watts Publishing Group Limited
Carmelite House
50 Victoria Embankment
London EC4Y 0DZ

An Hachette UK Company
www.hachette.co.uk
www.hachettechildrens.co.uk

Contents

Aisha and Emily are best friends from Spellford Village. Aisha loves sports, whilst Emily's favourite thing is science. But what both girls enjoy more than anything is visiting Enchanted Valley and helping their unicorn friends, who live there.

Silvermane

Silvermane and the other Night Sparkle Unicorns make sure night-time is magical. Silvermane's locket helps her take care of the stars.

Dreamspell's magic brings sweet dreams to all the creatures of Enchanted Valley. Without her magical powers, everyone will have nightmares!

Dreamspell

With the help of her magical friends and the power of her locket, Slumbertail makes sure everyone in Enchanted Valley has a peaceful night's sleep.

Slumbertail

Kindly Brighteye is in charge of the moon. The magic of her locket helps its beautiful light to shine each night.

Brighteye

Enchanted Cottage

Golden Palace

An Enchanted Valley lies a twinkle away,
Where beautiful unicorns live, laugh and play
You can visit the mermaids, or go for a ride,
So much fun to be had, but dangers can hide!

Your friends need your help – this is how you know:
A keyring lights up with a magical glow.
Whirled off like a dream, you won't want to leave.
Friendship forever, when you truly believe.

Chapter One
A Flight at Night

In her cosy bedroom, Aisha Khan and
her best friend, Emily Turner, were
getting ready for bed. Bright moonlight
shone through the small window under
the thick thatched roof of Enchanted
Cottage, and faraway stars twinkled like
magic lanterns.

"Today was so fun," Aisha sighed happily. "I still can't believe you get to stay for the whole week!"

"Me neither!" said Emily. "School holidays are the best. What shall we do tomorrow?"

"Hmmm," Aisha said. "You showed me how to make that brilliant baking soda volcano today, so tomorrow, maybe I could teach you how to play badminton?"

"Sounds great!" laughed Emily.

Their pyjamas were lovely and warm from the tumble dryer. Aisha closed the curtains and snuggled down in bed under her colourful patchwork quilt. Emily got into her blow-up bed on the floor.

Aisha's mum knocked and stuck her head in. "Teeth all brushed, you two?"

"Yes!" they said together.

"Faces washed?"

"Yes!"

"Good girls. Snuggle down, now. Goodnight! Sweet dreams!"

She switched off the light and closed the door.

A silver thread of moonlight shone in between the curtains.

"I hope we dream about Enchanted Valley," Emily whispered. Enchanted Valley was a secret magical world they were lucky enough to visit sometimes. Their unicorn friend Queen Aurora ruled kindly over all the creatures living there.

Aisha yawned. "Me too. Goodnight!"

"Goodnight."

A moment later, Emily sat up. "Aisha, where's that light coming from?"

Both girls looked around the room. Something on the bedside table was shining, making pretty, dancing shapes on the walls.

"It's our unicorn keyrings!" Aisha

whispered. Their treasured keyrings were
little crystal unicorns, given to them by
Queen Aurora.

"I bet Enchanted Valley needs our help!"
Emily whispered back.

The girls knew all was not well in
Enchanted Valley. The wicked unicorn
Selena, who wanted to be queen, had

stolen four magical lockets from the Night Sparkle Unicorns. Now Enchanted Valley was stuck in an endless night!

Emily and Aisha had already helped get the star unicorn Silvermane's locket back, but there were still three more Night

Sparkle lockets to find.

They both scampered out of bed and pulled on their fuzzy animal slippers – Aisha's were bunnies, Emily's pandas – and pressed their keyrings together.

Whoosh! Multicoloured sparkles swirled in the air as they were lifted gently off the ground, their hair floating around them.

As the sparkles faded away, their feet touched the ground again and they looked up in breathless excitement. Instead of Aisha's bedroom ceiling, the night sky of Enchanted Valley arched over them.

In front of them, Queen Aurora's golden palace glowed in the darkness, like a comforting light showing the way home. The eight turrets stood strong and proud, their spires reaching up to touch the blanket of stars.

Aisha and Emily walked towards the drawbridge over the bright blue moat

that surrounded the palace.

Clip-clop came the sound of hooves from up ahead. Queen Aurora came out to meet them, her glorious gold mane flowing behind her. Her body shimmered in all the changing colours of the dawn sun, and the silver crown shining on her brow was as delicate as morning dew. By her side walked the lilac unicorn, Dreamspell, who was in charge of sending lovely dreams to everyone.

"Queen Aurora! Dreamspell!" The girls gave them each a hug.

"Welcome back, girls!" Aurora bowed her head. "Thank you for coming so quickly."

"We always love coming here!" Emily

said. "But let me guess – Selena's been up to no good again?"

"I'm afraid so," Queen Aurora said. "She still has three of the lockets. It's very important that Dreamspell gets her locket back as soon as possible."

The girls remembered Dreamspell's special locket. It contained pictures of beautiful dreams. When they had first looked into it, they'd seen a birthday party, a sunny beach and a lovely picnic with friends.

"Oh dear, what's happened without the locket?" Emily asked.

Dreamspell said, "It might be easiest if I show you. Climb up on my back. I can fly you to where the trouble started."

She bent down, and Aisha and Emily climbed on. Aisha held on tightly to Dreamspell's shimmering lilac mane. Emily put her arms round Aisha's waist.

"Good luck," said Queen Aurora. "I shall stay and guard the palace, just in case Selena tries to take over."

Emily and Aisha waved goodbye as Dreamspell began to trot away.

"Hold on tight," Dreamspell said. "I'm a

fast flyer."

She galloped for a bit then leapt into
the air as if she were jumping a gate. But
instead of coming back down, she just
kept going up and up!

They went flying like a comet over
Enchanted Valley. Wind blew through the
girls' hair. The girls could see the palace
towers shining far below and the moat
glistening blue like a sapphire necklace in

the starlight.

"Wow, you're the fastest unicorn we've ever ridden!" whooped Aisha.

"I LOVE flying," Dreamspell called back. "Hold on, let's do a loop-the-loop!"

The girls clung on tight as the lilac unicorn soared up and over. They were upside down for a moment, with the ground above their heads as they zoomed round the loop. The girls cheered.

"I wish I had time to show you more," said Dreamspell. "But we need to hurry."

Rolling green hills spread out in front of them like a rippling sea. Further on stood the towering trees of the forest, dark and mysterious. Once they reached the forest, Dreamspell began to glide back down to earth. She headed for a little grove among the trees, where a pink and white house stood. The walls bulged out like plump cushions and the roof sat on top like a funny little hat. A delicious smell like toasted buns came wafting up from a tiny chimney. Colourful windows shone with welcoming light.

"That house looks like it's made of marshmallows!" Emily said.

Dreamspell landed in front of the house. Aisha spotted a sign hanging beside the door, in the shape of a fluffy rabbit. "*The Pufflebunny Inn*," she read. "*The Cosiest Night's Sleep You'll Ever Have!*"

"Tonight was supposed to be Petey the Pufflebunny's grand opening," Dreamspell told them sadly as they slid off her back. "Everyone was looking forward to spending a lovely night here. And then ..."

Whimpering and sobbing sounds floated out from inside the inn. From time to time one of the lights in the windows would go out, only to pop back on again moments later.

From the sound of it, nobody was getting any sleep at all!

"Oh dear," said Dreamspell. "It's getting worse!"

Chapter Two
Blueberry Bursts

Inside the Pufflebunny Inn, a warm fire crackled in the hearth. Everywhere the girls looked, they saw soft, comfortable things. Mountains of pillows and cushions had been piled up invitingly in the corners. Fluffy blankets were draped everywhere, ready to snuggle under.

Delightful smells of roses, lavender and
hot chocolate wafted through the air.

Emily admired a velvety purple
armchair. "This is the cosiest place I've
ever seen!"

"Petey the Pufflebunny has the magical
power to make everything cosy and
comfortable," said Dreamspell.

Just then, a frightened squeak came
from upstairs.

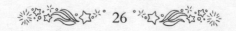

"That guest doesn't sound very comfortable to me!" said Aisha.

She sprinted up the wide wooden stairs, with Emily and Dreamspell following close behind. They found themselves in a long corridor, full of worried guests milling about.

A little otter in pyjamas stood outside his room, crying.

Aisha knelt down next to him. "What's

the matter?" she asked gently.

"I want to go home," sobbed the otter.
"I had a bad dream. A monster was
chasing me!"

"It was only a dream," Aisha
said soothingly, giving him a hug.
"Everything's all right now."

Then Emily noticed that further down
the corridor, there were more guests
looking just as upset. She spotted a
grumpy badger in a night mask, a family
of pixies who were all shivering in fear,
and a tiny dormouse in a pink nightie.

"What a horrid dream I just had!" the
dormouse told Emily. "I dreamed it was
raining day and night, and my house got
washed away!"

"I dreamed I was all alone in a scary forest," said one of the pixies, quivering.

"Is everyone having bad dreams?" Emily asked.

"Indeed we are," the badger said gruffly. "Nobody's getting a wink of sleep."

Dreamspell hung her head sadly. "I'm supposed to keep bad dreams away," she said. "But I can't without my locket. Poor Petey's opening night is ruined. I feel so helpless."

"It's not your fault," Emily cried. "It's that nasty Selena!"

"We're going to get that locket back, right away!" Aisha said.

But just then, a big, fluffy pale brown bunny came scurrying around the corner.

He looked just like one of Aisha's bunny
slippers, except that he was wearing a
fluffy dressing gown and carrying a silver
tray.

"Time for some sweet treats before
bed. Help yourselves!" the bunny called.
"Plenty of nibbles to go around."

On the tray were heaps of treats: iced

pastries and gumdrops, cherry pies and chocolate buttons, marshmallow puffs and tiny, delicate cakes.

"Oho," said the bunny as he spotted Aisha. "You must be Aisha and Emily! My name is Petey. I'm so glad you've dropped by. Hello, Dreamspell! Please, sit down."

Aisha and Emily sat on two gigantic gold cushions so soft they sank into them.

"I'm sorry your grand opening isn't going well," Aisha said.

Petey looked confused. "Not going well? Everything's going exactly as planned!"

Emily looked at the miserable guests and whispered to Aisha, "It doesn't look like it to me."

"It's nice of you to come, but you needn't have," Petey went on. "A nice sweet treat will sort out all those bad dreams, I'm sure of it."

Aisha stood up. "Well I hope you're right, but in the meantime, we're going to do our best to find Dreamspell's locket!"

Petey hopped up and down, holding out his tray. "Oh, do have a snack before you go. Please? I worked so hard baking them."

Aisha and Emily weren't very hungry, but they didn't want to be rude to the poor pufflebunny. They each took a bright blue gumdrop in a little nest of spun sugar. Aisha gave one to Dreamspell as well.

Petey beamed. "Blueberry Bursts! Excellent choice."

The gumdrops were unbelievably delicious. First there was the crunch of the spun sugar, then the gumdrop burst in their mouths with a juicy pop that made their tongues all tingly.

A moment later, Emily felt a drowsy, dreamy feeling washing over her. She closed her eyes happily and sank back into her cushion. She yawned and stretched. "I think I'll just rest my eyes for a moment before we go."

Dreamspell curled up on a soft rug. "It's funny. Flying doesn't usually tire me out like this ..." Next moment, she started to snore.

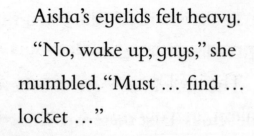

Aisha's eyelids felt heavy. "No, wake up, guys," she mumbled. "Must … find … locket …"

It was no good. She curled up against Dreamspell's warm flank, laid her cheek against her smooth lilac coat, and fell fast asleep.

The girls woke up, shivering in the cold. The warm, cosy Pufflebunny Inn had vanished. Now they were in a dark stone room. There were rusty bars in the windows, covered with tangled, creeping vines. Murky moonlight shone in.

The wall they were leaning on was filthy with dust and old webs. Aisha tried to pull herself away, but iron chains held her fast.

Her heart sank even more when she saw Dreamspell chained to the opposite wall. Petey the Pufflebunny was sitting next to her.

"Where are we? What happened to the inn?" Emily cried out.

Petey blinked. "Hello! Who are you two? Dreamspell, what are you doing here?"

Aisha felt very confused. "It's us, Petey! We were all at your inn a moment ago, remember?"

"But how can that be?" Petey frowned. "I've been locked up here for three days."

"But that's impossible!" Emily protested.

"It's true," insisted Petey. "I was making the beds, getting ready for my first guests, when Hettie the Hedgehog offered me a Blueberry Burst. I must have fallen asleep, because the next thing I knew, I woke up here. That was three days ago."

"Where is here?" Dreamspell wondered. "Where are we?"

The girls looked around. Even though it was a horrible place, something about the dingy room looked familiar …

"We've been here before," Aisha said. "Yes, I remember now! This is the tower

where Selena kept Wintertail locked up,
isn't it?"

With a shiver, Emily remembered the
time Selena had kidnapped the Winter
Festival unicorn, Wintertail, and stolen all
three of her lockets. Snowstar, Wintertail's
foal, had helped them get the lockets back
and rescue her mother.

Emily gasped. "But that means … we're

in Selena's castle! We must have been brought here in our sleep."

"We need to find a way out!" Aisha added.

Emily desperately looked around for some way out of the tower. But all she saw were dangling cobwebs drooping down, ready to drop into her lap, and spooky flickering candles on the wall. Outside, the wind howled like a lonely ghost.

She shuddered. Somehow, the tower had become even scarier than before!

Suddenly, thunder boomed above. Lightning flickered through the narrow tower windows. The door flew open and in came Selena!

Her silver body gleamed in the candlelight, and her mane and tail were the dim blue of midnight mists. On her head – to Aisha and Emily's horror – was  Queen Aurora's crown!

"Comfortable?" Selena laughed.

"Not really," Emily said, rattling her chains.

Selena snorted. "Too bad. Get used to it! You're my prisoners now. And I have my trusty friend here to thank for it."

A big pale brown rabbit in a dressing

gown came hopping up to her side. Emily and Aisha stared. He looked exactly like Petey, who was sitting opposite them!

"Good heavens," Petey exclaimed. "It's like looking in a mirror."

"You didn't tell us you had a twin brother," Emily said.

Petey looked very confused. "I don't!"

Emily and Aisha looked at each other in total confusion. *What's going on?*

Chapter Three
Captured!

Aisha frowned at the new pufflebunny. "Who are you?"

Selena's pufflebunny opened his mouth and screeched. Aisha and Emily covered their ears.

With a dark *whoooosh* of magic, the bunny vanished. In its place appeared

Screech the owl, flapping his wings and cackling!

Screech was Selena's latest servant. He had helped her steal the Night Sparkle lockets in the first place. He had the power to change shape to look like anything he wanted.

"Now I understand! You used your magic to look like Petey," Emily said. "We thought we'd met the real pufflebunny, but he was locked up here all along!"

Screech let out a hooty laugh. "Haha, that's right! Those Blueberry Bursts I worked so hard to make were really

Snoozy Chews!"

"No wonder we all fell asleep," Aisha groaned.

Selena pranced up and down. "Oh, clever, clever me. I've finally done it. I snatched the crown right off Aurora's silly head! Now you'll be trapped for ever while I rule over Enchanted Valley!"

"Aurora's the queen, not you!" Aisha shouted.

"Yeah!" Emily yelled. "And she always will be!"

"Those days are over!" Selena stamped her hoof on the floor. "I'm queen now. I've hidden Dreamspell's locket where nobody will ever find it. Aurora will never rule over this valley or see her precious friends ever again. And there's nothing you pesky little girls can do!"

Selena stomped out of the room. The door slammed shut. They all heard the clunk of a key turning.

"She's locked us in!" Petey wailed.

"It's going to be OK," Emily promised him.

"We need to get out of here," Aisha said. "But how?"

The room went quiet. The only sound was the moaning of the wind outside.

"I wish we could change our shape, like Screech," said Emily. "I'd turn into a mouse and slip out of these horrible chains."

"You poor girls look so uncomfortable

having to sit on the cold, hard floor!
I can't bear it," said Petey miserably.
"Would you like me to conjure up some
cushions for you?"

Aisha gasped. "Did you say conjure?"

"All pufflebunnies have the magical
power to make other people comfortable,"
Dreamspell reminded her.

"Magical, eh?" said Emily thoughtfully.
"I'm sure I'd be a lot more comfortable if
these chains were off. Do you think you
could fix them with your magic, Petey?"

"Oh, why didn't I think of that? Silly
old me!" cried Petey.

Petey puffed his cheeks and blew,
"Huffity puff!" like he was blowing a
dandelion clock. Sparkles of magic flew

from his mouth.

Aisha and Emily held up their hands. As the sparkles touched the chains, the chains changed into elastic hair scrunchies! The girls pulled them off easily.

The magic sparkles went on dancing around the room, changing whatever they touched. The rusty bars and tangly vines in the window disappeared and became pretty curtains, swaying in the breeze. The hard, stone floor was covered by a lovely patterned rug. The ragged cobwebs turned to fluttering butterflies, and the dangling chains were silky tassels.

"Hooray!" the girls cheered together. "We're free!"

Petey looked a little happier. "I'm afraid

we're not quite free yet. I can't unlock the door," he said.

"We'll just have to climb out of the window, then!" Aisha said.

They all gathered at the window and looked down. Far below the window lay jagged rocks and thorny bushes.

Emily gave a little gulp. "I forgot how high up we were."

Dreamspell laughed. "Have you forgotten how much I love to fly?"

Everyone excitedly climbed up on to Dreamspell's back. Petey sat in Aisha's lap.

Dreamspell stepped away from the window and took a deep breath. She rose a few centimetres off the ground … and sank right back down again. She took a deep breath then strained and tried again.

"Are you all right, Dreamspell?" Aisha asked.

"What's wrong?" said Emily.

"My worst nightmare's coming true," Dreamspell whispered. "I can't fly!"

Chapter Four
Comfy Jumps

Dreamspell's nostrils flared and her eyes were round with fright. "Why can't I fly?" she whimpered.

Aisha stroked Dreamspell's soft mane. "Don't worry," she said soothingly. "We'll figure it out."

"Yes, we will!" Emily said firmly. "But

right now we're going to have to think of another way out."

She slid off Dreamspell's back and peered down from the window. Then a brilliant idea popped into her head. "Hey, there are some great big thorny bramble bushes down there. They look really uncomfortable."

"Uncomfortable?" Petey squeaked. He hid his face in his paws. "Oh dear!"

"No, it's a good thing, Petey," Emily said. "Since they're so uncomfortable, perhaps you could turn those prickly bushes into big comfy pillows? Then we can jump down on to them!"

Petey's eyes grew wide. "Oh I see!" he cried. "In that case … huffity puff!"

And he blew!

More pufflebunny magic sparkles came shooting out, drifting down on to the bushes below like snowflakes. The bushes vanished, and a pile of plump white pillows popped up in their place.

"Well done!" The girls clapped.

They all gathered at the window. Aisha and Emily glanced nervously at each other.

"I'll go first," Aisha said, bravely.

She stepped up on to the window ledge and looked down. The pillows looked very small and far away.

"Here we go," she said nervously. "One, two, three …"

Aisha jumped. Wind whistled through

her hair as she fell. Then, with a *whoomph* like a duvet settling on a freshly made bed, she landed in the pillows.

"Phew," she gasped. "I'm fine, everyone! Come on!"

One by one, they all landed in the pillows and climbed out of the pile, laughing with relief.

The landscape was misty

and bleak, with withered grass all around, bare and crooked trees, twisty overgrown paths, and marshes bubbling in the distance.

Aisha and Emily looked up at the tower window high above their heads and grinned. "We did it!" cried Aisha.

"Now to find the locket!" Emily added.

Just then, something flew out of the window and zoomed down towards them. Something with big, angry, yellow eyes.

Screech!

"Get back in your cell, you miserable bunch!" he shouted.

"No!" said Petey, putting his paws on his hips and glaring.

"I'm telling Selena!" squawked Screech. "Then you'll be sorry!"

"No, we must stop him!" Emily yelled.

They all ran, galloped and hopped after Screech. He flapped away, hooting with laughter.

Aisha was a fast runner, but not fast enough. Every time she almost caught him, Screech darted out of the way. "Ha ha!" he teased. "Too slow!"

"I wish we had a net to throw over him," Aisha panted.

Petey took off his dressing gown and passed it to Aisha. "Will this do?"

"That's perfect!" Aisha said. "Thanks, Petey!"

The next time Screech swooped low,

she flung the robe over him. "Mmmf!"
he squeaked, trying to wriggle away,
but the robe was caught on some of the
remaining thorns. The more Screech tried
to break free, the more tangled up he got!

"Let me out!" hooted the struggling
lump.

Emily said, "Tell us where Dreamspell's
locket is and we'll let you go."

"Selena kept it with her," came the
muffled voice. "That means you'll never,
ever get it back. Queen Aurora will be a
prisoner at the Golden Palace for ever!"

Emily turned pale.

"Aurora is a prisoner?" Aisha gasped.

"That's right! Hoo hoo hoo!"

"My locket will have to wait," said

Dreamspell. "The queen is much more important. We must free her, right away!"

Petey bounded off across the withered grass. "This way to the palace. Follow me!"

They followed Petey up the slope of a hill. It was hard going. The grass was thick and tangled.

When they reached the top of the hill, they stopped and stared. Enchanted Valley stretched into the distance, lit by murky green starlight. But it was far from the happy place they knew. Everything had changed.

The orchards where apples had grown and birds had sung were now groves of silent, dead trees. The paths between the

meadows were overgrown and littered
with sharp stones. A few sad pixies tried
to gather wilted flowers in fields where
the ground was dry and patchy.

Aisha gasped. "Is this even Enchanted
Valley any more?"

"Cursed Valley is more like it!" Emily
said with a shiver.

"I can't understand any of this," Emily
frowned. "Selena must have done it, but
how?"

"She must be using Dreamspell's locket," Aisha replied.

"But my locket only has power over dreams, not the fields or the orchards," said Dreamspell.

"Maybe it's because she's made herself queen then?" said Emily in a small voice.

There was nothing for it but to keep going. The further they walked, the darker and more frightening their journey became. Twisted vines had grown over almost everything, and spindly-legged spiders with many shining eyes wove gloomy grey webs across their path. The friends picked their way through squelchy bogs and tangled thickets. Emily and Aisha held hands as they went.

Aisha groaned as her foot sank into yet another muddy patch. "This is going to take for ever!"

Just then, they smelled smoke, and a high-pitched shriek cut through the air. It was hard to see clearly in the darkness of the night, but they could just make out a row of lit-up windows moving steadily along.

A rickety old train was coming their way!

"It might be going to the palace," said Emily.

"If it will get us there quicker, we have to take it," said Aisha. "We must rescue Queen Aurora!"

Chapter Five
Out of Puff

"Look, there's a station over there," said Aisha, pointing. "Quick, let's run and catch the train!"

The four friends scrambled towards the run-down old train station. It was the most miserable thing they had ever seen in Enchanted Valley, after Selena's

castle. Half the tiles had fallen off the roof and long grass was growing up between the tracks. There was a cafe that might have been pretty once, but now it was all boarded up.

Two shabby little trains stood waiting at the station, billowing thick black smoke.

A crow in a scruffy, once official-looking blue cap wandered over.

He glanced warily at the friends. "Can

I help you?"

"We need to get
to the palace right
away," Emily said. "Can we
get there on one of these
trains?"

The crow chuckled.
"Either one will get you there," he said.
"One of the trains goes super-duper fast
but the other one goes very slowly."

"We'd like the fast one, please!" said
Aisha.

"Oh, you would, would you?" The
crow folded his wings. "We don't let just
anyone ride the fast train. You've got to
solve a riddle first – a tough one."

"I can do this," Emily whispered to

Aisha. Emily loved figuring out puzzles and riddles. After all, science was all about finding answers! She turned to the crow. "I'm ready."

"Right, then," said the crow. "A train leaves from Stinky Swamp, heading towards Tangle Town at one hundred kilometres per hour. Three hours later, a train leaves Tangle Town heading towards Stinky Swamp at two hundred kilometres per hour. If there are exactly two thousand kilometres between Stinky Swamp and Tangle Town, which train will be closer to Stinky Swamp when they meet?"

Emily frowned. Aisha could see her lips moving as she tried to figure it out.

"All the numbers are swirling around in my head," Emily moaned. "I can't work out the answer!"

Aisha squeezed her friend's hand. "You can do this, Emily. You're brilliant at puzzles."

"Not this one!" Emily sighed. "I'm sorry, Aisha. I can't even guess!"

"Don't feel bad," Aisha said. "I haven't got a clue either."

"Neither do I," said Dreamspell.

Petey's ears drooped. "Sorry," he said.

The crow let out a hoarse laugh.

"You fools! When the trains meet, they're at exactly the same place! So neither one is closer to Stinky Swamp!"

"Argh!" Emily put her head in her hands. "It's obvious. I feel so silly!"

"Me too," groaned Aisha. "It'll take ages to get to the palace now."

Dreamspell hung her head. "If only I could still fly."

They climbed on board the slow train. Petey conjured up some pillows and blankets to make the dingy seats more comfortable.

A whistle blew and the train lurched and puffed slowly along the track like an old, out-of-shape dragon going for a jog.

There was nothing to do but stare out

of the windows. The train trundled past empty houses with broken windows, where the wind made spooky noises as it howled over the chimney pots. It swayed its way past overgrown swamps, where hunched-over trees trailed vines in their path and clouds of smelly green gas hovered above bubbling mud.

Emily made a face. "This train may be slow, but I'm glad I don't have to walk through that!"

On and on chugged the lumbering train. Then, at long last, it came to a halt.

"Finally!" Aisha sprang to her feet. She threw open the door and bounded out on to the platform. The others followed.

"Oh no!" Dreamspell cried.

Aurora's lovely home looked like a crumbling old ruin. The golden rooftops were falling in, the walls were cracked and toppling and nasty green gunge was dribbling down the towers!

"We have to get inside and help Aurora," said Emily.

"But how?" Petey said. "Look. The drawbridge is up."

They all walked over to the stone ledge where the drawbridge usually lay. Now it was pulled upright by stout iron chains on the other side of the water. Normally, the moat was sparkling and crystal clear, but now it was muddy and murky.

"There's only one thing for it," Aisha said bravely. "I'll swim across the moat, climb up and lower the drawbridge for you all to cross."

Dreamspell nuzzled her. "Please be careful."

Aisha stroked Dreamspell's nose gently. "I'll be fine. I'm a strong swimmer."

She took off her bunny slippers and left them with Petey. Then she took a deep breath, swung her arms back and dived.

As soon as she hit the freezing cold
water, it started to churn and rush, like a
big river. Aisha kicked her legs and took
good strong strokes.

"Come on, Aisha!" Emily yelled
from the side. "You can do
it!"

Aisha swam as
hard as she
could,

but the current was growing stronger and stronger. The water buffeted her like a raging giant.

A wave washed over her head. Aisha spluttered, gasped and fought on. She had to keep going, but no matter how hard she kicked, she wasn't getting anywhere. She felt her arms and legs getting tired and before she knew it, she was being swept away! "Help!" she shouted.

Chapter Six
Friendship to the Rescue

Emily saw her friend being washed away and cried out in horror. "We have to save Aisha!"

Petey hopped to the edge of the moat and stretched his little paw out as far as he could reach. "It's no good, Emily. She's too far away!"

"If only I could fly!" Dreamspell wailed.

"I'm going in after her," Emily said boldly.

She was just pulling off her panda slippers, ready to dive in, when she saw the flash of a sparkling green tail gliding through the dark water. "It's Pearl!" Emily exclaimed.

Their mermaid friend was by Aisha's side like a shot. "Don't worry, Aisha. I've got you!"

She wrapped her arms around Aisha and towed her through the churning water, over to the far side of the moat.

Emily, Dreamspell and Petey all burst out cheering!

Aisha gave Pearl a tight hug. "Thanks

for helping
me, Pearl.
I don't
understand

what happened to the moat. How could
still water become so choppy and wild?"

"It's whatever horrible magic has settled
in Enchanted Valley," Pearl said, shivering.

"Selena's behind it," Aisha said. "She's
taken Aurora prisoner."

Pearl gasped. "How did she do it?"

"We don't know," said Aisha. She
climbed out, dripping wet and shivering,
found the drawbridge lever and pulled
it. With a loud rattle and bang, the
drawbridge crashed down. Emily,
Dreamspell and Petey came running over.

Emily hugged Aisha. "I was so worried!"

"Uncomfortable, my dear? We can't have that!" said Petey. Quick as a *huffity puff*, Aisha's hair was dry and her pyjamas were soft and warm again. Petey gave her back her slippers.

"Thank you!" Aisha sighed, putting them on. "That's much better."

"Now we'll find Queen Aurora and set her free," said Emily. "Then she'll put everything right again."

"Please hurry," begged Pearl. "Even I can't swim in water as rough as this for much longer. Good luck!"

She waved from the moat as the four friends headed into the creepy palace.

Their footsteps echoed in the huge, draughty entrance hall.

"Where do you think Queen Aurora might be?" asked Emily, peering around.

"I don't know," said Dreamspell, "but Selena's all over the place. Look!"

She pointed to the wall with her horn. From floor to ceiling, portraits of Selena were on display. Selena sitting in a throne, Selena lounging on a cushion, Selena admiring herself in a mirror, portraits in square frames, round frames, oval frames, large and small … they went on and on as far as the eye could see.

Aisha felt uneasy under the gaze of a thousand painted Selenas. One of the paintings showed Selena sticking out her tongue, and Emily bravely stuck hers out right back at it.

They crept on, making as little noise as

they could. Thankfully, the dust that had settled like a grey carpet muffled their footsteps.

"There're spiderwebs everywhere," Emily whispered and pointed at the ragged webs hanging down in every corner.

"It looks like nobody's cleaned this place in about a million years," muttered Petey.

"But these halls were gleaming like gold yesterday." Dreamspell sighed. "How did things go so wrong, so fast? It must be some truly powerful magic."

Aisha turned a corner and found her way was blocked by two tall glass doors, covered in dust. She tried to open them, but they were locked.

Through the misty glass she could make out the hallway beyond, where Queen Aurora kept all the paintings of the children who had visited Enchanted Valley over the years. The frames were still hanging there, but they were all empty.

And in the far corner sat Queen Aurora herself! But she was staring down at the floor, not moving at all. She looked lonely and sad, as if all hope had deserted her.

"Queen Aurora!" cried Aisha and Emily. They banged on the glass.

Aurora didn't move. It was as if she hadn't heard.

"Your friends are here to save you!" Aisha called as loud as she could.

Queen Aurora didn't even look up. "This is just another one of your cruel tricks, Selena," she said in a voice heavy with sorrow. "I have no friends."

"What?" Aisha gasped. "No friends? Why on earth would she say that?"

Emily pounded on the glass. "We're your friends!" she shouted.

"I don't believe you," Queen Aurora said sadly.

"We're going to have to get in there and prove it," Aisha said. "Can anyone see a key?"

It took only seconds of looking around before Petey shouted, "There!" He pointed to where the key was sitting. "Oh …" It was protected by a fat, furry spider.

"I'll get it," Emily said, bravely. "Selena must have thought spiders would scare us off, but they're actually really interesting, 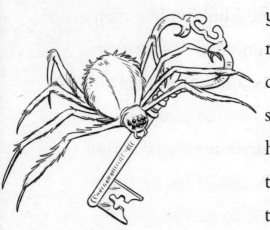 you know." She reached out and lifted the spider with one hand, grabbing the key with the other. The spider squirmed and Emily couldn't help shuddering a little as she put it down.

"Well done, Emily!" said Aisha. "Rather you than me."

She quickly slipped the key into the lock and turned it. Everyone breathed a sigh of relief as the door swung open.

Aisha and Emily charged down the hall towards Queen Aurora, who looked up in confusion. They threw their arms around Aurora's neck and hung on like they would never let go.

"It's going to be OK," Aisha said. "We're here now."

Aurora's eyes grew brighter. "Aisha? Emily? Is it really you?"

"Of course!" Emily laughed.

Aurora's whole face lit up. "Oh, it's so good to see you! Selena told me all my friends had gone away and left me. She said I'd be alone for ever and ever."

"We'd never leave you alone," Aisha promised.

"And we'll always come to help,

whenever you need us," Emily added.

Aurora closed her eyes and laid her head in Aisha's lap. "Thank you, girls," she murmured. "You're the best friends I could ask for."

Chapter Seven
What a Nightmare!

The girls were so relieved to see Queen Aurora looking happy again. Of all the horrible sights they'd seen in Enchanted Valley today, a lonely and heartbroken Aurora was the worst.

Dreamspell ran up to join them. "What happened to you, Queen Aurora?"

Aurora blinked in confusion. "Someone sent me a lovely package of Blueberry Bursts, so I ate some for a bedtime snack. Next thing I knew, I woke up here, and all my friends were gone. I couldn't even remember their faces. Can you imagine? A friendship unicorn with no friends!"

"Poor Aurora!" Aisha sighed.

"When I saw you, it was like waking from a terrible dream," Aurora said.

Aurora's words echoed in Emily's mind. *Like waking from a dream …*

"Of course!" Emily shouted. "The answer's been staring us in the face this whole time!"

"What do you mean?" Dreamspell said.

"Don't you see?" Emily began to pace

back and forth excitedly. "Everything that's happened since we woke up in that tower has been just like a bad dream! I'm brilliant at puzzles, but I couldn't figure out the train riddle."

"Yes! I love swimming, but I couldn't swim across the moat," Aisha said. "Aurora lost all her friends …"

"… and I couldn't fly!" cried Dreamspell. "You know how much I love flying."

"Everywhere I look I see uncomfortable things," Petey said with a shudder. "Sharp things, stony things … it's a pufflebunny's nightmare!"

"Exactly." Emily grinned. "A nightmare. We've all come face to face with our own

worst fears!
And all
the trouble
started
when we fell
asleep."

Aisha's mouth made an O. "But if we're all in a nightmare, that would mean ..."

"We're all still asleep!" finished Emily.

"So none of this is real?" Aurora looked around her ruined palace. "I do hope that's the answer!"

Emily clapped her hands briskly. "OK, Aisha, let's put our theory to the test! How can we tell if this is all a dream?"

Aisha thought hard. "Maybe we could try to run away from something?" she suggested. "Whenever something is chasing me in a bad dream and I try to run away, I can't get anywhere."

Emily nodded and bent down. "Petey, can you chase us, please?"

"I'm not very scary, but I'll do my best," Petey said. He held up his little paws, went "Rarr!" and chased after Aisha and Emily.

Both the girls tried to run away. Sure enough, it was like trying to run through thick glue. Their legs moved in slow motion.

"That answers that!" Emily said.

"Good thinking," said Aisha. "The only question now is, how are we all dreaming the same thing?"

"Hoo, hoo, hoo!" A laugh burst out from above them. They looked up to see Screech circling overhead. "You're so slow! You're all trapped in the same dream, of course!"

"But whose mind could be dreaming such horrible things?" asked Dreamspell.

"Selena's!" Emily burst out. "Why else would there be pictures and statues of Selena all over the place? This may be a bad dream for all of us, but for Selena it's the best dream ever!"

"That means Selena is asleep

somewhere too," Aisha added.

"With my locket!" said Dreamspell.

Petey rubbed his eyes. "This is all very confusing, I must say. If this is just a dream and we're all asleep, then where are we really?"

"It doesn't matter," Screech squawked. "Because you're never waking up!"

"We're in the same place we were when we fell asleep in the first place," Emily declared triumphantly, ignoring the owl. "The Pufflebunny Inn!"

It made Aisha smile to think they were really in that lovely, snuggly warm place and not in the crumbling palace. "Unless we get Dreamspell's locket back, the bad dreams will keep coming," she said. "So the first thing we need to do is wake up. Then we find Selena!"

"Let's pinch each other," Emily suggested. She saw the frightened look on Petey's face and added, "Not too hard, though. Just enough to wake us up."

"No, don't try that!" Screech yelled, swooping at them.

"Very well," Petey said, trying to sound brave. "Emily, Aisha, you pinch everyone, and then each other."

They all moved into their places.

"Stop it! Stop it!" Screech wailed.

"Will this work?" Petey asked nervously.

"Only one way to find out," Aisha said. "Here we go …"

Chapter Eight
Sweet Dreams

With a sudden start and a gasp, Aisha
woke up.

She sat bolt upright and looked around.
Thank goodness! They were back in the
cosy corridors of the Pufflebunny Inn.

Emily sat up next to her. Dreamspell
blinked sleepily and shook her tangled

mane out of her eyes. "What a relief," she sighed. "I never want to be stuck in a dream that bad ever again."

Emily cupped her hand to her ear. "Listen!"

From somewhere nearby came a dull *thump thump thump*.

"Let's go and see what it is," said Emily.

They ran towards the sound. Soon they found a little double door with a sign reading BROOM CUPBOARD. Someone had jammed a broom through the door handles.

Thump! The doors shook.

Emily quickly pulled the broom out and the doors burst open. There, gasping, with messy fur and a mop bucket stuck

on his foot, was Petey the
Pufflebunny!

Petey looked very
upset. "After Selena and
Screech put
me to sleep,
they must have
stuffed me in
here like an old
rag!"

The girls
helped Petey out, got the bucket off his
foot and gave him a cuddle.

Just then, a strange sound came
from upstairs. It was a sort of rattling,
rumbling, gurgling sound, a bit like a
cement mixer full of porridge.

Aisha froze. "What's that?"

"Let's find out," replied Emily.

Slowly, quietly, they climbed the twisting, turning stairs. The peculiar rumbling sound grew louder and louder the higher they climbed.

"It's coming from the master bedroom," Petey whispered. "The most comfortable room in my whole inn!"

Aisha gently pushed open the door.

There, tucked up in an enormous four-poster bed, was Selena. She was fast asleep, and snoring – that's what the noise was! Screech sat on the end of the bed, wearing a long white nightcap with a bobble on it. He was asleep too, muttering and moving his wings restlessly.

Selena rolled over. Her pyjamas had spiders on them, with big, happy smiles. She was holding on tightly to an old, scruffy, custard-coloured teddy bear with one button eye. Something was twinkling from around its neck.

Aisha moved closer to get a better look.

The teddy bear was wearing Dreamspell's locket! Aisha could make out a crescent moon shining inside it. As

she watched, the moon changed to a huge bowl of ice cream, then to a toy shop, then a patterned rug covered in sleepy kittens.

"We've got to get that locket!" Aisha whispered.

"We can't just grab it," said Emily. "She'll wake up."

Aisha tried gently pulling the teddy away, but Selena mumbled in her sleep and wrapped her front legs around it even more tightly.

"Perhaps I could take the bear's place," suggested Petey.

"Are you sure?" Aisha said. "I think it might be pretty … uncomfortable."

Petey looked determined and nodded, his ears flapping. "We have to get the locket back, whatever it takes!"

"Good luck!" Aisha whispered.

Petey hopped up on to the bed. He slowly nuzzled his way up beside Selena, pushing the bear out of the way. She mumbled again and squeezed him tight. Petey gave the girls a helpless look.

Aisha quickly snatched up the bear. She took off the locket and slipped it over Dreamspell's neck.

"Hurrah!" Petey squeaked.

"Mmm?" Selena stirred.

She looked dozily at the pufflebunny

cowering beside her and her eyes flew wide open. "What? You're not my teddy! Where's Mr Snuggy-Wugs?!"

At the sound of her shrieks, Screech suddenly woke up. The cap flew off his head. "Hoo! Hoo!" he yelled, beating his wings wildly. "Alarm! Intruders! Wake up, Selena!"

"Oh, be quiet, you useless bag of feathers," Selena snapped. "You're too late!"

She leapt out of bed and snarled at the girls. "How dare you take that locket from me? I was queen! How dare you ruin my lovely dream!"

"And that's all it'll ever be," Aisha said. "A dream."

"So long as we're around, it'll never come true," added Emily.

"I wouldn't be too sure about that," Selena said. "Don't forget, I still have two of the Night Sparkle lockets left. I'll be back, you meddlesome pests! Unpleasant dreams!"

She let out a wild laugh. Lightning

crackled through the air and a boom of thunder shook the inn to its rafters. The window blew open, and Selena and Screech flew out into the night.

The friends all walked back downstairs to find all the frightened little creatures back out in the corridor.

"Good news, everyone," Emily called. "Dreamspell has her locket back!"

All the creatures burst out cheering.

The girls turned to Petey.

"What do you say we restart your opening night?" Aisha asked him.

Petey hopped up and down with excitement. "What an excellent idea! Hot chocolates all round!"

"And then you will all have the sweetest

dreams you've ever had," Dreamspell
promised.

Everyone cheered again.

The girls stayed long enough to enjoy
a hot chocolate with their friends. Then,
as all the guests started to drift towards
their comfy bedrooms, they said goodbye

to Petey. Dreamspell flew them back to Queen Aurora's palace.

Queen Aurora came out to meet them. "It was so nice to wake up back in my lovely palace, with all my good friends still here," she said. "Thank you for helping us once more!"

Dreamspell smiled. "I can't wait to conjure up sweet dreams for everyone."

"You girls were very brave to stand up to Selena like that," added Queen Aurora.

"It wasn't just us," Aisha said. "We couldn't have done it without Pearl, Petey, and Dreamspell's help."

Emily agreed. "That's what makes dreams come true. Friends working together as a team."

Aisha yawned, and Emily did too.

Queen Aurora laughed. "Perhaps the two of you need some proper sleep."

"Good idea!" Emily said.

"I'm ready to go home and go to bed," Aisha agreed.

They walked to the top of a grassy green hill. "We'll be back to find the other Night Sparkle lockets!" Aisha called. "We promise!"

They hugged Aurora goodbye.

Aurora's horn began to glow bright as a lantern. Shining sparkles

appeared, swirling around Aisha and Emily. They rose even higher into the air than they had flown on Dreamspell's back.

Then, quick as a candle flicker, they felt themselves come back down into Aisha's room. All the familiar things of Enchanted Cottage were around them once more.

Aisha looked at her clock. No time at all had passed while they had been away.

She yawned and stretched. "I'm worn out after all those adventures!"

"Me too," Emily said. Then she added with a giggle, "But it's not the Snoozy Chews this time!"

They snuggled down under their covers and closed their eyes, each of them hoping they would dream about Enchanted Valley and all their wonderful friends.

The End

Join Emily and Aisha
for another adventure in …

Slumbertail and the Sleep Pixies
Read on for a sneak peek!

"Aisha?" whispered Emily Turner. "Are you awake?"

The duvet on the bed next to Emily's shifted, and her best friend Aisha Khan's face appeared. By the moonlight shining faintly through the curtains, Emily could see her grin.

"I've been trying to keep my eyes closed," Aisha whispered back. "But then I start thinking about unicorns, and I'm wide awake again!"

Emily giggled. "Me too!" The two girls were having a week-long sleepover at

Enchanted Cottage, where Aisha lived with her parents. They were in Aisha's bedroom, each snuggled under a cosy duvet.

"I tried counting sheep, but that didn't work," Emily said. "So then I tried counting unicorns. But that just made me wonder what Queen Aurora was doing!"

Read
Slumbertail and the Sleep Pixies
to find out what adventures are in store for Aisha and Emily!

Also available

Book Five:

Book Six:

Book Seven:

Book Eight: